ADDY'S WEDDING QUILT

ADDY · 1864

BY CONNIE PORTER

ILLUSTRATIONS DAHL TAYLOR

VIGNETTES SUSAN MCALILEY

THE AMERICAN GIRLS COLLECTION®

Published by Pleasant Company Publications
© Copyright 2001 by Pleasant Company
For information, address: Book Editor, Pleasant Company Publications,
8400 Fairway Place, P.O. Box 620998, Middleton, WI 53562.

Printed in Singapore.
01 02 03 04 05 06 07 08 TWP 10 9 8 7 6 5 4 3 2 1

Edited by Jodi Evert and Michelle Jones
Designed by Joshua Mjaanes and Laura Moberly
Art Directed by Joshua Mjaanes

Library of Congress Cataloging-in-Publication Data

Porter, Connie Rose, 1959-
Addy's wedding quilt / by Connie Porter ;
illustrations, Dahl Taylor ; vignettes, Susan McAliley.
p. cm. — (The American girls collection)
Summary: Though her parents "jumped the broom" to get married
when they were slaves, now that they are living free in Philadelphia
after the Civil War they plan to have a church wedding and Addy
works to complete a special quilt to give them as a wedding gift.

ISBN 1-58485-274-7
1. Afro-Americans—Juvenile fiction. [1. Afro-Americans—Fiction.
2. Marriage—Fiction. 3. Slavery—Fiction. 4. Quilts—Fiction.]
I. Taylor, Dahl, ill. II. McAliley, Susan, ill. III. Title. IV. Series.
PZ7.P825 Ag2001   [Fic]—dc21   00-033614

The
AMERICAN GIRLS
COLLECTION
®

PICTURE CREDITS

The following individuals and organizations have generously given permission to
reprint illustrations contained in "Looking Back": p. 40—Abby Aldrich Rockefeller
Folk Art Museum, Williamsburg, VA; p. 42—Slave quarters, photograph from *The
Strength of These Arms* by Raymond Bial, copyright 1997 by Raymond Bial, reprinted
by permission of Houghton Mifflin Company, all rights reserved; Broom, from
Collector's Illustrated Encyclopedia of the American Revolution by George C. Neumann
and Frank J. Kravik, courtesy George C. Neumann; p. 43—Copyright Robert
Holmes/CORBIS; p. 44—North Carolina Museum of Art, Raleigh, purchased with
funds from the State of North Carolina; p. 47—Photographs and Prints Division,
Schomburg Center for Research in Black Culture, the New York Public Library; p. 48—
Photography by Jamie Young, prop styling by Jean doPico, and craft by June Pratt.

TABLE OF CONTENTS

ADDY'S FAMILY
AND FRIENDS

ADDY'S FAMILY

POPPA
*Addy's father,
whose dream gives the
family strength.*

MOMMA
*Addy's mother,
whose love helps the
family survive.*

ADDY
*A courageous girl,
smart and strong,
growing up during
the Civil War.*

SAM
*Addy's sixteen-year-old
brother, determined to
be free.*

ESTHER
*Addy's two-year-old
sister.*

M'DEAR
*An elderly woman
who befriends Addy.*

MISS DUNN
*Addy's kind and patient
teacher, who doesn't
like lines to be
drawn between people.*

SARAH MOORE
Addy's good friend.

HARRIET DAVIS
*Addy's snobby desk
partner at school.*

ADDY'S WEDDING QUILT

Addy Walker sat on a small stool before the fireplace in M'dear's room, stitching together a quilt. The chill of evening draped over her back like a wet sheet. Shivering, she pulled her heartwarmer closer around her shoulders. Though her back was freezing, she had to wipe away sweat that rolled down her brow. Her brother Sam always said that sitting in front of a fire was like being caught between two seasons. Summer

1

was in your face, winter at your back.

Addy said, "When summer come, you ain't never, ever going to hear me grumbling about it being too hot."

M'dear was sitting in her high-backed rocker with a shawl around her shoulders. "Everything has its season, Addy. Even the cold."

"Well, I can't wait for this season to be over. It never got this cold in North Carolina. I wish I could go to sleep tonight and wake up when it's summer."

"Now, be careful what you wish for. If you did that, you'd miss your folks' wedding next week. Would you want to do that?" asked M'dear.

"No, ma'am. I been working too

hard on this quilt! I hope they'll like it."

"I'm sure they will," said M'dear. "Let me see it."

M'dear was blind, but she had her ways of seeing. Running her long, thin fingers over the quilt squares, she nodded her approval. "Your work is much better," M'dear observed. "These new stitches are small and tight."

Addy smiled. She had been sewing for weeks, ever since Momma and Poppa had announced their wedding plans. They had wed twenty years earlier on Master Stevens's plantation, but they had not been married in a church.

During slavery, that was against the law. Like many slaves, Momma and

*M'dear was blind, but she had her ways of seeing. Running her long,
thin fingers over the quilt squares, she nodded her approval.*

Poppa married by simply jumping over a broom. M'dear, who claimed to be older than dirt, had told Addy she had even jumped the broom when she married "eleventy-seven" years ago.

Addy had no money to buy Momma and Poppa a wedding gift, so she decided to make one. In the family trunk, Momma kept fabric to make a quilt. With all the sewing Momma did for other people, she never found time to make it. Addy decided to surprise Momma and Poppa by making it herself.

Standing up to warm her back, Addy said, "These squares I done today is from Uncle Solomon's shirt." She let out a spiritless sigh. "It's going to be such a nice wedding, but I don't feel all-the-way happy because him and Auntie Lula didn't live to see it."

"I know you miss them," M'dear said. "One of the best things about quilting is that every piece of fabric can be a reminder of the past. It's a way of remembering people, not with sadness, but with love." She asked Addy to take a quilt of hers from the foot of her bed.

"I made that quilt after my husband died," M'dear explained. "Most of the squares are from his clothes." Addy admired the fine stitching and the cut-outs M'dear had sewn on. There were cutouts of a cabin, a man standing next to a horse, horseshoes, and an apron.

"I'd like to put some cutouts on my quilt," Addy said.

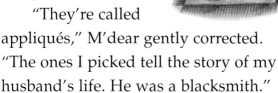

"They're called appliqués," M'dear gently corrected. "The ones I picked tell the story of my husband's life. He was a blacksmith."

"I don't know what to pick for Momma and Poppa," said Addy.

M'dear said, "You don't have to choose them all at once. Start with one that you feel says something important. The others can come later."

That night while Addy lay in bed next to Esther, she thought about what appliqués to make. For Momma she could make one of a spool, or a needle.

For Poppa's job as a carpenter, she could cut out a hammer or saw. But none of them seemed just right. The more Addy thought, the more she knew she probably wouldn't have time to add them before the wedding anyway.

The next morning she was taking the quilt to school so Miss Dunn could write her parents' names and the new wedding day in fancy script that Addy would embroider over. Addy had never embroidered before, and Miss Dunn said she would teach her. She was even giving Addy the embroidery silks!

Addy smiled as she thought of spending time after school with her teacher. Miss Dunn was so smart. Her words were as smooth and polished as pearls. Addy wanted to be like her when she grew up. As much as she looked forward to their time together, she felt bad telling Momma a half-truth the next morning.

Addy told her, "Miss Dunn need to keep me after school today."

"Why?" Momma asked. She was making Addy's lunch, a biscuit with bacon grease. "Things going good at school, ain't they? You ain't having no trouble with Harriet again?" Momma asked. She added a wizened apple to Addy's lunch.

"No, Momma!" Addy insisted. "Miss Dunn got

9

some special project she want me to help her with." Addy didn't look directly at Momma. She fiddled with her knee warmers.

"I guess it'll be all right," said Momma. She handed Addy her lunch pail, telling her, "You make sure you come right straight home."

Thanking Momma with a quick hug, Addy grabbed her school sack and gave Esther a kiss that Esther promptly wiped off. Then Addy tiptoed into M'dear's room, tucked the quilt under her coat, and headed off to school.

As much as Addy liked school, she was eager for this day to end. In the afternoon the class took turns reading

aloud. Addy lost her place while waiting
her turn. Her seatmate, Harriet, was
sneaking raisins from her pocket.
Students weren't allowed to eat during
class. Miss Dunn would make Harriet
stand in the corner if she caught her, or
if Addy told. For a few moments, Addy
thought about telling. The delicate sweet-
ness of those raisins teased her, making
her hungry for a treat she couldn't have.
Momma and Poppa had no money to
buy treats. Addy felt that if she did have
a snack—a sleek, sweet bit of taffy, a
delicious salty tidbit of jerky—Harriet
would probably blab it from here to
China. But Miss Dunn always said not
to be a tattletale, so Addy decided not to

tell. Besides, when the school day ended, she'd have the treat she wanted—spending time with Miss Dunn.

✷

Addy let out a long "Oooh" when Miss Dunn showed her the embroidery silks. For Addy, holding them was like having a rainbow in her hands. Sitting next to Miss Dunn, Addy watched her stretch the center of the quilt over a large embroidery hoop, pulling the cloth taut until its surface was flat. Then Miss Dunn added the top hoop, tightening it in place with its small screw. Carefully, she began writing,

dipping her pen into the inkwell on her
desk, blotting the extra ink before she
wrote on the cloth. When the teacher
finished, Addy admired
the fancy writing.

"I hope I can make my
stitching look as nice as
your writing," Addy said.

"Sure you can," Miss Dunn encour-
aged her. "You're a fast learner."

Miss Dunn started a few stitches at
the top of the loop in Momma's name.
The cloth was pulled so tight in the hoop
that each time the needle poked through,
Addy could hear a tiny popping sound.
Halfway around the loop, Miss Dunn
handed the needle and thimble to Addy.

13

Miss Dunn made sure Addy's stitches weren't too tight or too loose.

"Take your time. If you work steadily all week, you'll finish in time for the wedding," Miss Dunn assured Addy.

Addy wasn't so sure. She would have to work both neatly and quickly if she wanted to add appliqués, too. For now, she went slowly. She knew the embroidery silks were expensive, and if she made mistakes, she couldn't cut the stitching loose and start over, as she could with ordinary thread.

While Addy worked, she glanced up now and then to see Miss Dunn going about her tasks—banking the fire in the stove, putting seats atop desks, erasing the blackboards and wiping them clean with a wet rag.

"I never knew you did this much work after school," said Addy.

"Wouldn't it be wonderful if elves came every night and did my chores!"

"If I had elves helping me, I'd have them do my long division," Addy laughed.

"Yes, but life isn't a fairy tale," Miss Dunn said. "I have to finish quickly. I have a meeting in a few minutes."

"I'm not an elf, but I can help you with your chores," Addy volunteered. "You been so nice, helping me with my quilt, giving me the silks. Besides, if I'm going to be a teacher one day, I better get used to the chores."

15

Smiling, Miss Dunn thanked Addy and told her what needed to be done. Then she left for her meeting.

Addy took the quilt to her desk and quickly went about the chores. She brought in kindling to start the fire in the morning, swept the floor, and placed each seat back in place. Then she stood and looked at the room. An army of elves couldn't have done better work, Addy thought. To celebrate a job well done, Addy laid the broom down and jumped over it, again and again, making up a song.

Soon as I miss, I'll know this.
There'll be a letter, sweet as a berry,
For the name of the boy I will marry!

Addy called out a letter of the alphabet each time she jumped. She had gotten
to *J* when she saw Harriet enter the room.
Addy was so surprised that she tripped
over the end of the broom.

"How long you been spying on me?"
asked Addy as she got to her feet.

"I wasn't spying," Harriet said. "Spies
hide. I was standing right in the doorway
long enough to know you're going to
marry a boy whose name begins with *J*."

Anger warmed Addy's face, but she
spoke in an even tone. "I was just playing."

"It didn't seem like it," Harriet said.
She walked over and picked up the
broom. "Maybe this is trying to tell you
that you're going to marry Joshua."

Addy called out a letter of the alphabet each time she jumped.

18

"Never!" Addy protested, snatching the broom. "You're going to marry him."

"Not me! I don't know if he'll ever marry if he doesn't stop picking his nose."

Addy burst out laughing and Harriet joined in. Addy put the broom down, and Harriet went over to the double desk she shared with Addy. She read the writing on the quilt. "That date is next week!" Harriet exclaimed. "Your parents aren't married?"

"My folks got married on the plantation a long time ago. Now they gettin' married in freedom," said Addy. She picked up the quilt. "This a secret. I'm giving it to them for a wedding present."

Harriet said, "Seems like more than that quilt should be a secret. After all, your parents aren't married."

"You take that back!" demanded Addy.

"There's nothing to take back. It was illegal for slaves to marry," said Harriet.

Addy was silent. All she could do was look at Harriet. She didn't know if what Harriet said was true.

She told Harriet, "My momma and poppa jumped a broom, so they married."

Harriet took a book from her desk. Then she ran to where the broom lay on the floor. She jumped over it. "Look, I just married myself," Harriet teased.

"It's not funny!" Addy said angrily. "You going to have to marry yourself,

because no one is going to want to marry
you, not even Joshua. I'm jumping the
broom when I get married."

"No, you're not, because that's a slavery way of doing things. Slavery ways
should be left in the past. In slavery."

"Jumping the broom is not a slavery
way," Addy said.

"I only came to get the book I forgot,
not to argue with you. Nobody jumps the
broom these days because it was wrong
in the first place. It never meant any-
thing," said Harriet. To prove her point,
she jumped the broom again, skipped
past Addy, and turned to give her a self-
satisfied smirk as she disappeared out
the door.

As Addy walked home from school, she wondered if Harriet was right. Addy thought, *If Momma and Poppa really is married, why they getting married again?*

Addy decided to ask M'dear. But M'dear wasn't feeling well, so Addy worked quietly beside her as she napped in her rocker. Still, that question kept bothering her. She couldn't get it out of her mind. It kept her from concentrating, so she went to find Momma. Momma was hemming a dress while Esther was playing on the floor with her doll. Addy sat down and halfheartedly played with her sister.

"Is everything all right, Addy?" Momma asked.

Addy took a deep breath and asked, "Why you need to get married in a church?"

"Poppa and me *want* to get married in a church," Momma said.

"Is there something wrong with jumping the broom?" asked Addy. "Was it just slavery ways?"

"Who been filling your head with them thoughts?" asked Momma. "Harriet?"

Addy's eyes grew big. In one long breath, she spilled what Harriet had said.

Momma put her work down. "First of all, Harriet should keep her nose out of other folks' business," she said. "As much as I hate to say it, she may be right. Jumping the broom was what folks did in slavery. There wasn't nothing wrong with it. It's just that now that I'm in freedom, I want to do what I couldn't then—stand up in church, say my vows, read me and your poppa's name on a real marriage certificate."

Addy smiled, knowing Momma would be pleased with the words on the quilt. Still, Addy had to be sure. She asked, "Did jumping the broom count? Harriet say it didn't mean nothing."

Momma turned Addy's face to hers. "You know something, Addy, in the Bible it say a man and wife is to be together until death part them. When you got married in slavery, they left that part out because your master could part you, sell you one from the other anytime he wanted. So me and your Poppa never had them words spoke over us. But we had that broom, and when we jumped it, we knew we belonged to each other for life.

"Maybe that don't mean nothing to Harriet. It mean a whole heap to me. I think it mean something to you, too, or you wouldn't have brung it up. You need to know your own mind, Addy. Harriet might know all there's to know in a book, but she don't know your heart. She don't know how you feel, so don't let her or nobody else tell you how you feel."

Addy told Momma, "I told Harriet I was going to jump the broom when I grow up, and she laughed at me."

Momma said, "I think it's sad that nobody jump the broom no more. You should've seen me. I jumped so high!"

"I want to jump the broom," Esther squealed. She got up from the floor and jumped up and down.

Momma and Addy laughed. "What about Poppa?" Addy asked eagerly.

"Y'all poppa jumped real high, too. If you stepped on the broom, you'd have bad luck." Momma let out a happy sigh, remembering. "I was so happy on my wedding day. Poppa looked handsome, and Auntie Lula made a big supper for everyone. She made dandelion greens, hog's head cheese, sweet cornbread, and

strawberries. The important
thing was we was together
with no master or overseer.
Uncle Solomon and the other
men sang and somebody played a banjo.
Everyone danced and danced.

"I had more sad days in slavery than
I can count, but that day was one of the
happiest. I cried because I was happy and
because I felt free. I felt free." Momma
sighed again and went back to her sewing.

☀

The next day, Addy hurried to finish
her homework before supper. Then she
hurried to M'dear's room to work on her
embroidery. She had finished everything

but "Walker" on the first line. She could do it and "Wed" the next day. Then all she would have left was the date.

Lying in bed that night, Addy thought she might even have time to make an appliqué. She could take the quilt to school and work on it during recess. All she had to do was think of something to add. But what? Just as she started falling asleep, she had the perfect idea.

"I got it," she said aloud.

"What?" asked Esther, who was lying next to her. "Can I have some?"

"You go to sleep," Addy said.

"You go to sleep," said Esther.

Poppa's voice boomed, "Y'all both go to sleep!"

At recess the next day, Addy sat at her desk, working on the quilt while the class went out to play. She carefully basted on the appliqué she had decided on—a broom.

As she worked, some girls came back into the classroom. They were heading to warm themselves by the stove when Harriet's friend, Mavis, turned to see what Addy was doing.

"That's real nice," Mavis said. "You did all this work yourself?"

Addy answered, "I did have some help, but I did all the sewing."

The other girls came over. Addy's best friend, Sarah, said, "Oh, Addy. Your

momma and poppa gonna love this."

"You're lucky your momma is a seam-
stress. She gets nice scraps," Mavis said.

"She do," Addy answered. "But these
all come from my family." She was telling
them she had gotten the broom handle
from one of Poppa's old cuffs and the
broom straw from a hem of Momma's

dress when she looked up to see Harriet standing over her.

"So, you're still making that slavery quilt," Harriet declared.

"It ain't a slavery quilt," Addy snapped at her, feeling that same rush of anger she'd felt when Harriet surprised her after school.

Unwrapping her long white scarf from her head and neck, Harriet said, "It is. Why else would it have that stupid broom on it?"

Just then Miss Dunn walked in. She came over to see Addy's progress. "Why, isn't this wonderful! I'm sure the broom will mean a great deal to your momma and poppa."

Harriet chimed in, "If you ask me, slavery ways should be left in slavery."

"Well, I didn't ask you," Addy blurted out. "But you can think what you want. I know how I feel. This here is a quilt about my family, Harriet." She pointed to the appliqué. "This is for my momma and poppa. It's true they married in slavery, but they really was married. This broom is part of the story of my momma and poppa's life, and I'm the one telling it."

Miss Dunn said, "Well, I don't think I could've said that better myself. Slavery is over, Harriet. It is in the past, but memories like these are about who our families are, who *we* are. Addy's right to cherish them."

The girls nodded quietly.

"So, now I'm asking you, Harriet, do you agree?" Miss Dunn asked firmly.

Harriet mumbled a quiet "Yes, ma'am."

The day of the wedding was beautiful. Momma wore the navy wool dress she wore to church every Sunday. It was plain, but Momma trimmed it with a collar and cuffs of crisp white linen. She pinned a small lace veil to her hat. Poppa had a new collar on his shirt, and his face was shaved smooth.

Reverend Drake told Momma and Poppa what words they should repeat.

Poppa said his with a firm, sure voice.
When Momma came to the words "Till
death do you part," she cried. With a
trembling hand, she pulled a lace hand-
kerchief from a cuff to dry her eyes.
Addy was sitting next to Sarah. Addy
was crying, too, and Sarah gave her
hand a reassuring squeeze.

At the wedding supper, Addy sat
between Sarah and Miss Dunn. They ate
ham, hoppin' John, collard greens, hog's
head cheese, and sweet cornbread with
strawberry preserves. For dessert they had
pound cake flavored with rose water, and
ice cream with pieces of candied walnuts.

Momma and Poppa opened all the
gifts during dessert. They loved Addy's

quilt. Poppa wanted to know when she'd found time to make it. Momma read her and Poppa's name. She read the date, and Addy smiled when Momma praised her stitching.

Addy took the quilt to the table where M'dear was sitting so she could see it. "I don't know if you can tell,"

35

Addy said, guiding M'dear's hand, "but this is a broom."

M'dear ran her fingers around its border. "Sure is," M'dear said, "and it's a fine one."

Addy knelt near M'dear. "You know something," said Addy, softly. "I'm not sad today, not even a little. Auntie Lula and Uncle Solomon would've loved this wedding. I feel all-the-way happy because I know they was happy when Momma and Poppa jumped the broom. I know something else, too. I know what appliqué I'm adding on next."

"You do?" M'dear asked.

"Yes, ma'am. You see, the broom, well, that's for the past. Next I'm adding the church. That's for today, and you know something? I like them both."

CONNIE PORTER

At 9   Now

I'm delighted to see that some African-American couples are making jumping the broom part of their wedding ceremonies again. I feel like Addy because I like both the church service and jumping the broom. If I ever marry, I'd like to jump as high as Addy's momma when she jumped, and find a husband nimble enough to jump just as high!

Connie Porter is the author of the Addy books in The American Girls Collection.

LOOKING
BACK
1864

A PEEK INTO
THE PAST

WEDDINGS IN 1864

When Addy was growing up during the Civil War, it was not legal for enslaved people to marry. The governments of Southern states thought of slaves as property, not as people or families. Still, enslaved men and women like Momma and Poppa got married anyway.

Many enslaved couples "jumped the broom" at their wedding. The couples were careful

This couple may be jumping the broom.

not to touch the broom with their feet. If they did, it meant trouble would come between them. After the ceremony, they weren't given a legal marriage certificate, but to their friends and families, and to themselves, they were married.

A marriage certificate from a legal marriage

Enslaved couples usually had to ask their masters' permission to marry. This was especially true if the man and woman were from different plantations. But masters usually gave their slaves permission to marry. Many masters thought their slaves would be happier if they were married. They also thought that the family ties would keep the slaves from running away.

An enslaved couple's wedding often took place in the slave quarters. Some ceremonies were very simple. One woman remembered her master saying, "Now you and Lewis wants to marry, and there

The slave quarters on a plantation

ain't no objections, so go on and jump over the broomstick together and you is married." In other ceremonies, a black preacher or a fellow slave read the vows. Afterward, there might be a big dinner with everyone singing songs.

Some masters thought of their house servants as part of the family. Sometimes the master's wife even organized a wedding for a house servant. The ceremony might have been held in the "big house" or out in the yard. The mistress sent invitations to friends and relatives and to the plantation owners who lived nearby. She might have even given the bride one of her old dresses to wear. The vows were read by a white preacher or the master, and after-

The "big house" on a plantation

*An enslaved couple's wedding celebration
in the hotel where they worked*

ward there was a big feast.

Tempie Herndon and her husband
were slaves on different plantations.
They had a big wedding on Tempie's
master's porch. The preacher from the
plantation church read their vows, then
they jumped over the broom.

Tempie remembered that Master

George held the broom about a foot off the floor. He told Tempie and her husband that the one who jumped over the broom backward and never touched the handle would be the boss. If they both jumped over the broom without touching it, there wouldn't be any bossing!

Although these ceremonies helped enslaved couples feel married, slaves were still the property of their owners. When there was money to be made, owners would separate families without hesitation. Just like Addy's family, many husbands, wives, and children were torn away without even a chance to say good-bye. This was one reason why many masters and preachers left the words "Till death do you part" out of slaves' wedding vows.

When the Civil War ended in 1865, it was legal for black people to marry in the South. Couples who had been separated by slavery searched for each other and legalized their marriage vows once they were reunited. For former slaves, getting married "by the book" was a sign of true freedom. One woman said, "My husband and I have lived together 15 years and we wants to be married over again now." In the South, many large wedding ceremonies took place in which 50 or 100 couples were married at the same time.

Former slaves also gained other rights after the war. They could legally learn to read and write, own property,

A wedding ceremony after the Civil War

and become U.S. citizens. But the most
important freedom for former slaves was
that they had control over their family
life. Finally, black people no longer lived
with the fear of being separated. They
had the freedom to be a family.

MAKE A
LOVE-LY PILLOW

Sew a pillow for a special friend.

When Addy found out that Momma and Poppa were going to get married in a church, she wanted to make something special for them. She decided to make a quilt using fabric scraps that Momma had saved. Addy added appliqués that told the story of Momma and Poppa's past as well as their future.

Make a pretty pillow as a gift for a celebration or just to show a friend how much she means to you. Use fabric scraps that have a special meaning, just as Addy did.

YOU WILL NEED:

 An adult to help you

Paper

Pencil

Fabric scraps

Straight pins

Scissors

Needle

Embroidery floss

Beads and buttons for decoration (optional)

Thread

2 squares of fabric, each 14$^1/_2$ inches

14-inch pillow form

1. Use the paper and pencil to make your patterns. Draw 2 hearts, each a different size. Cut out the hearts.

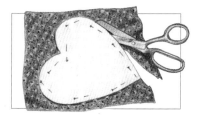

2. Pin one heart pattern to one of your fabric scraps. Cut around the heart. Do the same with the other pattern.

Step 3

Step 4

3. Center the small heart over the big heart and pin them together. Then use 2 strands of embroidery floss to sew the hearts together with a ladder stitch.

4. To sew a ladder stitch, come up at A and go down at B. Come up at C and go down at D. Keep going. When you've finished, tie a knot close to your last stitch, and cut off the extra floss.

5. If you like, sew beads and buttons in a design on the hearts.

6. Pin the hearts onto one of the large squares of fabric. Sew the heart appliqué to the fabric square with the ladder stitch. This is the front of the pillow.

7. Place the "right" sides of the fabric squares face-to-face. Pin them together.

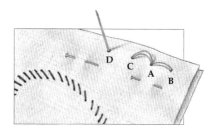

8. Use the thread to sew a backstitch around 3 sides, about ¼ inch from the edge. To sew a backstitch, come up at A and go down at B. Come up at C. Then go down at A and come up at D. When you've finished, remove the pins, tie a knot close to your last stitch, and cut off the extra thread.

9. Turn the pillow right-side out. Place
   the pillow form in the pillow. Fold
   in the edges of the last side and pin
   them together.

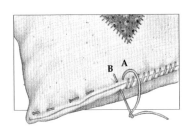

10. Sew up the last side with a whip-stitch. Bring the needle up at A, and then pull the thread over the edge to come up at B. When you've finished, remove the pins, tie a knot close to your last stitch, and cut off the extra thread.